# MAGGIE'S CURSE

# MAGGIE'S CURSE

## Debbie Poole

Spooky Moon

First published 2003 by Spooky Moon, an imprint of
Books Noir Ltd

www.booksnoir.com

ISBN 1–904689–08–4

Printed and bound in the UK

# Contents

# Contents

# Chapter 1

## *Summer Holidays*

Robbie Brown sat at the breakfast table, spooning his cereal into his mouth so quickly that he had no sooner swallowed one mouthful of cornflakes than he was chewing another.

"Robbie, take your time! You'll give yourself a tummy ache eating so fast," exclaimed his mother.

Mrs Brown tried to look severe, but she could see that her son was too excited to take any notice of her today. It was always the same on the first day of the summer holidays. Robbie would most certainly have all sorts of activities planned for the next six weeks and would probably spend most of his time out of doors. She wasn't worried that he would get up to any mischief, however, as in the small village where they lived, on the banks of Lake Trenton, all the local people kept a watchful eye on the children of the village. If they were seen doing something they shouldn't, or if they were in any danger, it would not be long before their parents were told about it.

"I have to be quick – everyone will be waiting for me in the park," spluttered Robbie through his cornflakes.

"Well, I'm sure they won't go anywhere without you . . ." but just as his mother spoke, the doorbell rang, and Robbie jumped out of his seat and ran to answer it. Mrs Brown could hear the rabble of several young boys as they argued about what they were going to do on the first day of their holiday, so she went out to the hall to remind Robbie about what he was not allowed to do.

Four other local boys were now standing in the hall around Robbie, chattering away, each adding his suggestions of things to do.

"Hello, kids. What are you planning to do today?" asked Mrs Brown.

There was a small chorus of "Hello, Mrs Brown" from the small flushed faces, and it was then that she noticed a little girl standing at the back, shyly trying to keep out of sight.

"Hello, there!" said Mrs Brown. "I haven't seen you before. Come in, and Robbie can introduce you properly."

The dark-haired little girl stepped forward, her face pink with embarrassment at being the centre of attention.

"That's Tessa, Mum," said Robbie. "She's Tommy's cousin, and she's staying with his family for the holidays, but we're going to try to find some girls for her to play with, because we're going ghost hunting and she'll be too scared, so she can't come."

Spots of anger appeared on Tessa's little round cheeks, and she glared at Robbie. "I've been ghost hunting before, and I wasn't scared then!" she said angrily.

Mrs Brown watched in amusement as the tiny girl squared up to Robbie, who was not amused at a girl standing up to him in front of his friends, but Tommy Mitchell, whose mother owned the local shop, pulled his cousin back.

"Tessa," he said irritably, "girls play with

dolls, and boys do the scary stuff. Everybody knows that, and you're only here 'cause Mum made me bring you, so you'd better behave or when we find the ghost, we're going to run away and leave you with it!"

Tessa looked slightly worried but remained defiant. "There's no such thing as ghosts anyway, so I'm not scared."

"Well, children, where are you going to hunt for these ghosts?" asked Mrs Brown, thinking she had better intervene before young Tessa beat up both Tommy and Robbie.

"Down at the Priory," Robbie immediately answered his mother.

"Well, I'm only going to say this once, Robbie," said his mother, "so listen very carefully. I don't want you going down to the lake, or to Maggie's stream. If you want to go swimming or fishing, then we'll make arrangements to have a grown-up there, but I don't want you near the water, and that includes boats and messing around on the piers. If I catch you, then I'll keep you in for the rest of the school holidays, and I'm sure the rest of your friends have all been told exactly the same thing by their parents."

Robbie knew better than to argue with his mother when she gave him this lecture, the same speech she made to him every summer. All the local children were told the same thing – there had been lots of swimming accidents in the lake, and Maggie's stream had claimed the lives of several children over the years. No one knew how the accidents had happened, as the stream was too fast-flowing for swimming and there were never any fish in it. In fact, there were no real attractions for children, but nonetheless the parents in the village always warned their children from going there.

"Don't worry, Mum. We're only going to the old Grainger graveyard. If there are ghosts, that's where they'll be."

Mrs Brown smiled at the serious expression on Robbie's face. She herself did not believe in ghosts, but she could see no harm in the youngsters looking for adventure.

"Okay, then," said Mrs Brown, handing Robbie a package of sandwiches she had made earlier. "Now, have you all got something to eat for lunch?"

The children nodded their heads.

"I'll see you when you get hungry again then. Be careful!"

The children all waved goodbye and made their way through the village. When they reached the Scout Hall, they decided on which route they would take to get to the graveyard, which lay in the grounds of the Priory.

The Priory was a huge old house near the shore of Lake Trenton. It had been the home of the Grainger family for many generations, and although it was now open to visitors, there were still Graingers living in it.

To reach the Priory grounds the children had to go past a gatehouse, where a gatekeeper lived. The children called him Frankenstein, after the scientist in the horror film who created a monster. Frankenstein did not seem to like the children playing down at the Priory. He would often come out of his house and just stand and watch them. Although he never talked to them, all the local children were frightened of him. He just looked scary, with his shining bald head, piercing blue eyes and lined face.

Robbie and his friends tried to walk past Frankenstein's house without looking back at the ever watchful eyes, but they all in turn felt a tingle in the back of the neck and turned to see that stony face and the sharp eyes boring into them.

"Why do you think Frankenstein hates kids so much?" asked Stephen Palmer. At ten years old, he was a year younger than Robbie. A chubby, red-haired boy with freckles, and a temper to match, always getting into scrapes, Stephen would argue about anything, but when he was in the mood he could be great fun.

"My dad told me that he only watches us, so that if anything gets stolen or damaged in the grounds, then he will know who is responsible," answered Robbie, who had spoken to his father about the old gatekeeper on several occasions. His father had always told him that although there were no laws saying that people could not explore the grounds around the Priory, Mr Bowman, which was Frankenstein's real name, did not like it, because of vandalism and damage to the garden ornaments, flower beds and fences that were all around the house. His father also told Robbie not to make any mess and to respect other people's property, and then there would be nothing Mr Bowman could do to stop him playing in the grounds of the Priory.

"Try not to make too much noise," Robbie now advised the others. "We don't want to give Frankenstein any reason to chase us. For all we know, he could be a kidnapper, or worse, or maybe he throws naughty children into Maggie's stream, and that's why so many kids have drowned there. You'd better watch out, Tessa, because I've heard he especially doesn't like little girls."

Robbie stared into Tessa's frightened eyes, feeling a little guilty for trying to scare her, but he was still annoyed that they were stuck with a girl. If he was nasty to her, he thought to himself, then maybe she would ask Tommy's mother to let her stay with her in future or she would find some other girls to play with.

14

The children continued on down the road, each of them a little disturbed by the presence of the grumpy old gatekeeper and keeping quiet so that he would not think that they were a gang of noisy vandals and and decide to follow them.

Soon the road began to narrow. On either side of it were huge bushes and trees that almost completely blocked out the sun, making it cold and dark, and creating an eerie silence, the kind of quiet that makes you want to whisper instead of talk out loud.

"Keep a look out for the gate. We should be at it any second now," said Peter Collins, who, at twelve, was the oldest of them all. He spoke in a low whisper and pointed to the rhododendron bushes to the right side of the road. "The bushes are getting thicker every year. It's no wonder nobody ever comes here! They might never find their way home again."

Tommy turned to look at him. "Peter, why are you whispering?" he asked. "I don't think Frankenstein can hear us any more."

"It's best not to disturb the spirits. If we make

too much noise then they might not appear," answered Peter, still in a low tone.

Nobody argued with him. The silence, the cold, the darkness amongst the trees, and what Peter had said about getting lost, was beginning to make them all feel a little scared, although none of them would admit to any such thing!

The children soon found the little wooden gate at the side of the road. Although well hidden by foliage, underneath the weeds and grass there was a hint of a path leading to the gate. The path continued through the gate and on into a wood. The path was very narrow and sometimes barely visible, but the children knew that to stray from it could mean getting lost. Taking their time, therefore, they managed to follow its route, winding through the dark creepy pine trees. The only sounds were the dull thuds of their footsteps on the carpet of twigs and pine needles and the sighs of their breathing, made louder by the silence as they made their way through the wood.

# Chapter 2

# *A Hidden Presence*

The disused graveyard was at the very back of the wood, and after walking for some time the children eventually reached it. The graveyard had once been the burial ground of the Grainger family, who had lived in the Priory house for generations, although no one had been buried there for over a hundred years. It was hidden inside a walled enclosure, with a huge cast-iron gate that creaked in protest as Robbie pushed it open and the children entered the graveyard beyond.

The wall of the graveyard went all the way around it, with another gate at the opposite side. The wall was crumbling in places, and the weeds and grass were so overgrown that some of the gravestones were actually concealed, but despite its lack of maintenance, the place had a very peaceful beauty, and after the dark wood, the children felt it a welcome change to feel the sun beating down into the enclosure. No trees grew inside the wall, letting in both heat and light.

At one side of the graveyard was a large tomb, with the names of the people who rested there carved into a huge plaque on its side. It was also inscribed with their dates of birth and death.

"Look how young some of these people were when they died," said Jamie Bennett. "There's hardly anyone over fifty here!" Jamie was in Robbie and Tommy's class at school, and the three of them had been best friends since they started school.

"Yes, and most of them are younger than thirty!" Robbie was good at maths, and it hadn't taken him long to calculate the ages of the people inside the tomb. "I wonder why so many Graingers died so young?"

"Mick says that the Grainger family had a curse on them, and because of that a lot of them had terrible accidents, and some even committed suicide, so now their ghosts still walk around in this graveyard because they are still cursed and can never go to Heaven!" Tommy excitedly relayed the tale that his big brother Mick had told him.

It was Mick who had first taken Tommy to the graveyard, and he remembered how scared he had been when his older brother had told him of the curse of the Graingers. They had seen no ghosts, however, and as this was the first summer that his mother had let him hang around with his own friends without Mick to keep a watchful eye on him, he had decided to investigate the old graveyard further and suggested to his friends that they come ghost hunting.

"That sounds like a lot of rubbish to me. Mick was probably just trying to scare you!" snorted Jamie.

Just as he spoke, a gust of wind swept through the graveyard, and with it a sound, like laughter – a child's laughter.

Tessa moved closer to Tommy. "What was that?" she asked.

"It's just the wind carrying sounds from the

lake. There are a lot of families picnicking there at this time of year," Tommy reassured her.

It had sounded a lot closer than that, but Tommy didn't want Tessa getting too scared. His mother had told him to look after her, and he would be in big trouble if Tessa told tales of ghosts and ghouls.

"Look over here!" Robbie was standing in front of a gravestone that had been cleared by the sudden gust of wind of the dead weeds that had previously hidden it.

The others went over to investigate. It was the grave of Margaret Grainger at the head of which stood a white marble cross with an inscription:

"Margaret Grainger
Born October 24th 1870.
Died suddenly August 19th 1879
Beloved Daughter of James and Anne
Grainger."

There was also a little poem:

"Darling Little Angel
I Think Of You Each Day

And Hope At Last In Heaven
You Found A Friend To Play."

All the children were silent for a moment, lost in their own thoughts, each wondering about the little girl who had died so young and what the sad little poem meant.

"She was almost ten, just like you, Tessa. I wonder how she died," said Tommy, feeling a little sad. He felt that the adventurous spirit of the day had gone now as he looked at the gravestone that stood out so much from amongst the others. He bent down to get a closer look, then something caught his eye. He pulled some of the weeds away and pulled out a little doll's shoe. It was very old-fashioned, similar to ones worn by the porcelain doll that his mother had in her bedroom. His mother had told him that the doll had belonged to his great-grandmother and was very valuable. He held the shoe out to the others.

"Do you think this is hers?" he asked.

"Whose?" said Stephen.

"Margaret Grainger's," replied Tommy.

Jamie looked closely at the little shoe. "It looks old enough, but surely if it had been lying here for all these years it would have been buried much deeper," he said.

Robbie knelt down in front of the grave and began pulling away more weeds and grass. "Maybe! Let's see if there is anything else," he said.

Stephen and Tommy helped Robbie to search while the others began to look around the surrounding area for anything else that might be connected. By the time they were ready to eat their sandwiches, they had found nothing, but after lunch they resumed their hunt.

Their efforts were fruitless, however, and after some time the afternoon sun began to dim, which meant it was time to go home. They would just have to come back tomorrow and look some more.

Robbie was the last out of the graveyard, and when he turned to close the gate behind him a shiver ran through him. He had a sudden feeling that someone was watching him. He paused and looked around to see if there was anywhere for someone to hide inside the wall, or maybe at the other gate, but he could see nothing. With a shrug, he pulled the heavy gate behind him and ran to catch up with the others, not hearing the laughter that echoed quietly round the graveyard.

By the time the children reached the centre of the village it was almost six o'clock. They had been at the graveyard all day, so they hurriedly said goodbye and went their separate ways, agreeing to meet in the swing park after dinner in the hope that their parents would let them out again after coming back so late from the graveyard.

At the Mitchell table, Tommy's mother asked Tessa what they had been up to, and Tessa launched into a tale of curses and graves and little girls who had died young. Fortunately, her excited babble didn't seem to concern Mrs Mitchell too much. She was just glad that her young niece had enjoyed herself and had not been given too hard a time by Tommy. He had been threatened with all sorts of nasty tasks before he would agree to let his cousin go with him in the first place, but she would have to tell him not to frighten her too much with his ghost stories. She didn't want Tessa to have nightmares.

"Tessa, you know there are no such things as ghosts," said Mrs Mitchell, "and the Graingers still live in the Priory – they don't seem to have a curse on them. In fact, Mrs Grainger was in the shop this morning, and she was telling me about one of her sons who is a famous film director."

"But, Aunt May, all the people in the graves were Graingers, and they died really young, especially Maggie!" exclaimed Tessa. She was sure there was a mystery surrounding the graves, and she so wanted to be included in the whole adventure.

"Maggie?" questioned Mrs Mitchell. She looked at Tommy, who could see that his mother was annoyed at him for telling his cousin about the curse.

"Maggie's just the name on one of the gravestones, Mum," said Tommy. "Tessa's just getting a bit carried away. We didn't say she was cursed. It's just some stupid story that Mick told me, and I was just telling the gang, but nobody really believes it."

He glared at Tessa. He was going to have to teach her what to tell parents and what not to tell parents, or, even better, get rid of her all together. Maybe Peter's little sister, Melanie, would take her off his hands. He would have to speak to him this evening.

Peter soon put paid to Tommy's plan, however, when the boys met again after dinner. "Melanie has gone away with her friend Deborah's family for a week, so it looks like you're stuck with her. Do you want a game of football tonight?"

"Listen, guys," said Tommy, "my mum gave me a big lecture about scaring Tessa after dinner tonight, so could you not mention all the scary stuff in front of her, because it looks like I'm stuck with her, or I'm spending the summer mowing the grass and painting the shed."

"Well, since she's not here," said Robbie, "why don't we talk about the scary stuff just now. It's maybe good that she's with your mum tonight because I didn't want to say anything in front of her, but there was definitely something in that graveyard today."

Robbie had decided to tell the others of the feeling he had had when he was leaving the graveyard earlier. All the others gathered round as he talked of his experience.

"Did you actually see anyone?" Stephen asked, but they all seemed to believe him, because none of them laughed, but then it had been a very strange day and each of them had felt a presence in the small enclosure.

"No," said Robbie, "but I can't describe it. When I was closing the gate something made me look across to the other side, and although I couldn't see anyone I'm sure someone was watching me. I just felt a chill and goose pimples up my arms. I really think someone else was there the whole time that we were."

Robbie shuddered as he remembered the feeling that had come over him when he was on his own, the last to leave the graveyard.

"Maybe it was Frankenstein?" Jamie suggested.

"Maybe," said Robbie hesitantly. "I don't know, but it's strange. I had the same feeling when we were reading the poem, like there was something other than us there, listening, watching. I didn't say anything at the time because I thought I was imagining it."

"I don't think you were imagining it, Robbie," said Tommy. "I felt a bit strange then too. I thought it was because the poem was so sad, but it really made a shiver run through me." He looked at the others. "I don't think we should go back there," he added.

"I thought we were supposed to be ghost hunting!" Stephen Palmer snorted. "Now maybe we've found one, and you're too chicken to even investigate. What can it do to us? There are five of us. I say we should go back tomorrow and let it know – whatever it is – that we know it's there, and then see if it comes out where we can see it!"

Jamie voiced his agreement. "Stephen's right. This is what we wanted. It would be stupid to stop going now that we are so close to finding a real ghost, or are you all too frightened?"

27

Tommy, Robbie and Peter immediately began to deny being scared, and before long they were arranging what time they would meet on the following morning for a return visit to the graveyard.

# Chapter 3

# *A Return Visit*

"Mum," said Tommy at the breakfast table next morning, "why don't you take Tessa to the shop this morning. I'm sure there are a million things she could help you with."

Tommy was using all his charm on his mother to persuade her to keep his cousin with her, so that he did not have to take her with him to the graveyard.

"Now, Tommy! Tessa should be getting fresh air during the holidays and not be cooped up in the shop all day, so be a good boy and don't argue or I will take you both to the shop."

"But, Mum——"

"I said no!"

Tommy knew not to push any further, so with one final glare at Tessa he made his way to the front door, with his annoying cousin skipping cheerfully after him.

As they were approaching the swing park to meet the others, he turned to Tessa.

"I'm warning you, Tessa," he growled, "if you get scared, I'm not going to take you home, and you'd better not tell Mum and Dad anything when we go home. Okay?"

"I promise, Tommy. I won't say a word. Cross my heart," she reassured him.

Tommy just tutted and walked away, muttering to himself.

"I see you've got your shadow with you again today, Tommy," joked Stephen.

"Ha, ha! Very funny," grumbled Tommy.

Once again the children crossed the fields and strolled down the long driveway. This time Frankenstein was nowhere to be seen as they passed the gatehouse.

"Maybe he's hiding in the woods, waiting for us," Peter whispered.

"Don't be daft. He's probably in the Priory grounds," Robbie scoffed.

"But, Robbie, what if it was him watching us

yesterday. You said there was someone there, and he wasn't at the gate when we came back up the road," said Peter.

"Shush!" warned Tommy. "Remember, little girls have big ears!" he added with a glance at Tessa, who immediately retorted, "I do not have big ears!" Spots of red anger appeared on her pink cheeks, and she stared defiantly up at Tommy.

"Never mind fighting, you two. We're wasting time," said Robbie marching away, leaving the others to follow.

Remembering the eerie wood, this time the children took the long way round the wood to reach the graveyard. There they stopped outside the graveyard wall, and with a worried look at the others, Robbie pushed open the gate and stepped inside.

He had not realised that he had been holding his breath until he saw that everything was just as they had left it the day before, and he let out a long breath in relief. There were no ghosts or monsters, just a little bird perched on top of a gravestone, Margaret Grainger's gravestone, just sitting there looking curiously at the band of worried-looking youngsters.

As they approached the stone, the little bird flitted away.

"Well, there doesn't seem to be much ghostly activity here today," said Jamie. "Maybe you were just imagining it, Robbie."

Robbie glanced around the quiet little burial ground. "Why don't we check the wood out," he said. "Maybe there's something in there to give us a clue. If someone was in there yesterday then he or she would leave footprints, or maybe someone is there just now and we will hear them."

"What if there's a ghost in the woods, or a werewolf, or even worse a murderer!" exclaimed Peter Collins excitedly. Peter watched a lot of scary movies and believed in all the monsters.

"Didn't you bring your monster-slaying kit with you, Peter?" asked Stephen Palmer, who was always the first to make fun of the others. The previous Christmas Peter had sent away for the ultimate monster-hunting kit from one of his ghost comics, much to the amusement of his friends who had ribbed him about it ever since.

"You can laugh, Stephen," replied Peter forcefully, "but some of those things really work. Let's just hope you never come across a werewolf or a vampire – you would be a gonner!"

"Yeah, right, Peter. Like you've fought vampires with your plastic cross and a clove of garlic, and then run home when you heard your mum calling you for supper, and the village being so full of vampires, you have a long way to go before your work is done," scoffed Stephen.

The argument continued for some time until Robbie exclaimed: "Look, Stephen, leave Peter alone! If we don't start looking soon we'll never know if there is a ghost or not, so let's split into two groups. If you find anything, shout and we'll all come running." He turned to Tommy. "You come with me, and we'd better take Tessa as well."

"Okay," replied Tommy, turning round to call his cousin. "Come on, Tess! Tess? Where on earth is she?"

Tessa had disappeared. Tommy looked stricken. What if something had happened to her . . . He began to shout her name, and the others joined in, but there was no answer.

While the boys had been engrossed in Stephen and Peter's heated exchange, they had all forgotten about Tessa, who had been wandering over towards Maggie's grave when something attracted her attention. At the open gate on the other side of the graveyard was a little girl about the same age as her. She was motioning to Tessa to come over, so without a word Tessa went over to see who she was.

As she approached the other girl Tessa glanced back uncertainly to where the boys were still arguing, but the little girl put her finger to her lips to indicate to Tessa not to tell them what she was doing, and she took Tessa's hand. Tessa found herself being led out of the walled enclosure and into the woods.

"Hi!" said Tessa to the little girl. "I'm Tessa, and my cousin Tommy is going to kill me for not telling him where I'm going."

The little girl just laughed and said, "But it's

only a game, hide and seek. We can leave some clues, and it will be such fun to see if your cousin can find us, and I know all the best places to hide."

"Do you live here, at the Priory?" asked Tessa.

"Sort of. Are you from the village?" The little girl asked, turning and studying Tessa. She seemed very pleased at finding someone to play her game with her.

"No. I'm here on holiday," replied Tessa. "My mum's having a baby, and everybody thought it would be best if I stayed with my aunt until the baby is born. My mum's very tired and my dad's working, but I will be going home as soon as the new baby comes. Mum says she will need my help."

Tessa was very excited about the prospect of a new baby brother or sister. She chattered on about how she couldn't wait for her dad to come and collect her as soon as the baby was born, as the little girl led her deeper and deeper into the wood.

# Chapter 4

# *The Search for Tessa*

"She can't be far," said Robbie. "Let's go this way."

Robbie made his way towards the back entrance beyond which the trees guarded Maggie's stream, Tommy following behind him. The trees were much thicker on this side of the graveyard, and, unlike the other wood, there was no trace of a pathway. Very few people ever ventured into it, as it was easy to get lost. Once they were inside, within moments the two boys soon found they had no idea which direction they were heading in or if Tessa had come this way.

"We must stick together, Tommy," said Robbie. "You don't want to get lost on your own in here."

The wood was so cold inside that Robbie

could actually see condensation when he spoke, his warm breath hitting the cold air. It was hard to believe that beyond the trees it was a clear summer day.

"How could Tessa have come in here on her own, Rob?" asked Tommy. "She just wouldn't. She even sleeps with the light on, and it's really dark in here. The minute she realised that she would have come back." Tommy had a bad feeling that something terrible had happened to his cousin.

"Maybe she's playing a joke on us," said Robbie, trying to reassure his friend. "Perhaps she's hiding, waiting to jump out on us. She might not have come this way, but the others will shout if they find her first."

Although he was trying not to make his friend worry, Robbie also felt that something was really wrong. He had been sure there was someone watching them the day before, and he had a strong feeling that they were not alone now.

The two boys had been walking for about ten minutes when they noticed something hanging from a low branch. Robbie retrieved it and handed it to Tommy. With sinking hearts, the boys saw that it was a red hair-band, and it was definitely Tessa's . . .

Immediately they began to shout for her, but there was no answering call.

"Do you think something has got her?" Tommy turned to Robbie, his face chalk-white and his hands shaking with a combination of cold and worry.

"I don't know, Tom," replied Robbie. "All we can do is keep searching, and if there's something in these woods, then eventually we'll find it, and if we're gone too long then I'm sure the others will get help."

Robbie prayed that this was the case, but he had no idea where the rest of the gang were or if they were safe. Would they be able to get help on time?

Suddenly a piercing scream ripped through the trees.

"Tess!" cried Tommy, trying to guess from which direction the scream had come.

"We'll have to split up," called Robbie, ignoring his own earlier advice. "Shout out if you find her, and I'll find you, and the same goes for me. Tommy, keep shouting if you get lost, and we'll find each other."

Robbie had taken command as Tommy looked as if he might panic, but they had no choice – the scream they had heard had sounded as if Tessa might be in danger, and they would probably find her more quickly if they split up. The two boys ran off in different directions.

Robbie forced his way through thick branches that scratched his face and tore his clothes, but he kept going, heedless of the pain. He could hear the flowing stream and knew that he was almost at the edge of the wood.

Sunlight was beginning to seep through the trees as they grew thinner, and he could see an exit, so he speeded up and ran through it, out on to the thick grass and weeds that grew along the bank of the stream.

Blinking his eyes as they adjusted to the sudden bright light, Robbie could make out a figure about ten metres away, hanging on to a dead tree at the side of the water, trying to reach something in the water. It was Tessa!

"Tommy, help me! She's going to drown!" he yelled, in the hope that Tommy would hear him.

"Tessa!" he called to the girl. "Don't move – the tree is coming away from the ground," he shouted in warning, but it was too late. The tree suddenly began to sway and fall. With a terrified scream, Tessa fell into the water and was dragged downstream by the fast-flowing current.

Robbie started to run along the bank, trying to keep Tessa in his sight. If he lost her now, who knows how far the water would carry her, that is if it didn't drag her under.

They were in luck. Tessa was caught up in some branches that were hanging into the water, and before the current could pull her away again unexpected help was at hand – Frankenstein, leaning from the bough of a tree, was reaching down into the water and hauling her out.

By the time Robbie caught up with them, the

gatekeeper had laid Tessa down on the bank and was leaning over her, looking concerned as she choked out dirty water, coughing and spluttering but still trying to speak, pointing towards the stream and gesturing frantically.

"Its okay, Tess. You're okay. You're safe now," said Robbie, falling to his knees beside Tessa and trying to soothe her.

"No! You have to get her out! She'll drown!" Tessa struggled to get up, but Frankenstein gently held her down.

"Its okay, lass, there's no one in the water," soothed Mr Bowman.

Robbie couldn't believe that this gentle man was the same man of whom they had all been so afraid, and he had saved Tessa's life!

# Chapter 5

# *Where's the Other Girl?*

Soon afterwards Tommy and Stephen came running out of the wood and along the bank of the stream. By now Tommy had been through so much that he was speechless at the sight of his cousin lying on the ground. She had obviously been in the water. What on earth was she playing at, he thought to himself. His mother had warned them to stay away from the water. He was angry with her for causing them so much worry, not to mention his journey through the woods in search of her.

Every sound had scared him witless. He could see nothing, and yet he felt a presence with him, like something ghostly chasing him, trying to scare him, but he had just kept running blindly, not knowing where he was going until he had found himself back at the graveyard. He knew he couldn't go back into the dark trees, so he had stood and shouted until Peter, Stephen and Jamie had found him.

"What's happened? Did you find her? Is she all right?" They had gathered around him, firing questions at him, but he was shaking and out of breath, and none of them could make sense of his story.

"Slow down, Tommy! What was in the woods?" Stephen had held him by the shoulders in an attempt to calm him.

"I don't know," answered Tommy, "but there's something in there. Sometimes it's as if the wood is alive. There is always the feeling that something is watching you, chasing you. We found Tessa's hair-band, and I knew she wouldn't go in there by herself, so we kept looking. Then we heard her screaming, so we split up, and I ended up back here, and I'm sure someone was following me. I heard noises. I'm even sure someone was laughing at me." Tommy looked at the others and whispered, "It could be watching us right now."

At that the others immediately started to

whisper, looking around them to see if they could see any signs of someone in the trees.

"Do you think Robbie might have found Tessa?" asked Stephen.

No one answered.

"I think we should get help," said Peter, who knew that adventure was one thing, but two of them were already missing, and if Tommy's face was anything to go by they were all in danger. It was perhaps time to get some grown-ups involved.

"There might not be time for that," said Stephen. "I think we should split up. Two of us should go for help and the other two should look for Rob and Tess."

Stephen didn't want to go into the wood after what Tommy had told them, but if they could stop anything happening to his friends then they had to do it.

They all looked at each other, none of them feeling brave enough, but none of them willing to let Robbie down when he needed them.

"Tommy, do you think you could show us which direction Robbie took?" asked Stephen.

Tommy looked totally dazed, and Stephen wasn't sure if he would be any use in the woods, but he was the only one who might be able to find the others.

"I don't know," answered Tommy. "It's really dark, much thicker than the other wood. I think Robbie headed off towards Maggie's stream, so we may be able to hear the water when we get closer, but it's really hard to know if you're going the right way once you're inside."

Tommy wasn't sure if he would be any help, but he had to try, and with any luck Robbie had already found Tessa and they would soon all be on their way back home.

"Right!" said Stephen, taking command. "Does everyone know what he's doing? Jamie, you and Peter get to the big house as quickly as you can. Phone your mum and tell her what has happened, but if there are any workers or other people at the Priory, you have to get them here fast. Tell them we're heading for the stream, okay?"

Stephen had made himself leader, and Jamie and Peter didn't argue. They just took off as fast as they could in the direction that led to the road.

Soon afterwards Stephen and Tommy took a deep breath and entered the woods that would lead them either to their friends or to the thing that had chased Tommy through the trees.

Immediately they were inside the woods Stephen turned to Tommy, whispering, "No matter what, don't stray. Even if something scares you we have to stay together, okay?"

Tommy nodded. Stephen wasn't absolutely convinced about Tommy's story of his flight through the woods. Not that he thought Tommy was lying, but he was beginning to think that they all might have been a little carried away, and now their imaginations were running wild. He half believed that there was a perfectly logical explanation for everything that had happened, and that they would soon all be laughing about their spooky experience, but still he kept glancing around him anxiously, just in case something caught him unawares. No matter how much he persuaded himself that there was no monster in the woods, his heart still pounded, and his stomach was in knots with nerves, as he let Tommy lead him through the dark trees, and he gave a silent prayer that they would find the others safe, and would soon be on their way home.

Every so often Tommy stopped and tried to listen for the sound of the water. Every time he stopped he also listened for sounds of someone following them, but the woods were silent, which was good, but they still had to get to the other side.

Eventually they heard the welcome sound of the stream, and they began to relax as the trees thinned out and they hurried towards the sunshine. Once out in the open they witnessed the scene of Frankenstein and Robbie with the bedraggled Tessa. They ran over to them to find out what had happened.

Tessa insisted that she had not been on her own. She kept saying that the reason she had fallen into the water was because she had been trying to reach in to save her friend, the same friend who had led her through the woods to play hide and seek.

Unfortunately, the other girl had disappeared beneath the water and Tessa had herself fallen in when the tree she had been gripping on to had come loose, and the next thing she knew she was lying on the bank with Mr Bowman and Robbie standing over her.

"Tessa, I didn't see anyone else," said Robbie. "Are you sure your friend fell in? Maybe she's just hiding from you."

Robbie had found Tessa after her friend had fallen in, but he had seen no one in the water, and Mr Bowman had also said he had seen no one.

"She fell in the water," cried Tessa yet again. "We were running along, and she went too close to the edge, and I tried to help her, but I couldn't reach her, and then she was gone!"

Tessa burst into tears and sobbed uncontrollably. Tommy kneeled down beside her, his earlier anger completely gone, and put his arm round her. "It's okay, Tess. Maybe she has been pulled further downstream. Peter and Jamie have gone for help. It's going to be okay."

"But she could be drowned, Tommy, and I

didn't save her. I wasn't big enough!" Tessa choked out the words as she tried to stop the tears.

Stephen and Robbie looked on helplessly. How awful! Where was this little girl's parents, and who would have to tell them their daughter might have drowned? All the warnings about playing near the water really hit home, and in a way they were glad that it was not one of them whose parents would be told of a terrible accident. Robbie thanked god that Frankenstein had arrived when he did, or it might have been Tessa's.

# Chapter 6

## *Robbie's Plan*

It was a very subdued Robbie who sat at the table with his parents that evening. Not that he had got into any trouble – his parents were just relieved that all the children were okay, and they could see that he hadn't really disobeyed them – he had only tried to rescue Tommy's little cousin.

They were all, of course, banned from going down to the Priory, and Mr Bowman had promised to let all the parents know if any of them tried to visit the old graveyard.

Robbie thought that Mr Bowman had acted quite strangely, as if he wasn't surprised when Tessa told her story about the other girl. He thought that Mr Bowman had seen more than he would admit. He even suspected that Mr Bowman had even been following Tessa. It was strange how he seemed to be right at the same spot when she fell in.

Even stranger than that was the little girl who, Tessa swore, had fallen in the stream. Priory workers and local police had searched the stream and found nothing. They had also interviewed people staying in the area, and nobody knew anything about a missing child. There had been no missing children, and everyone was completely puzzled by Tessa's story. It had even been suggested that Tessa had an imaginary friend and that she should maybe be taken to a doctor who specialised in such things.

Robbie's mother had talked to Tommy's mother on the phone, but his mother had been talking in a hushed voice so Robbie couldn't hear what she was saying.

He went to his room and gathered his thoughts. Something wasn't right. Tessa had been sure she was with someone. Although she didn't know the name of the other little girl, she had described her, and, as Tommy had said, there was no way she would have gone into the dark woods by herself. Frankenstein had said there had not been anyone in the water, but he had not looked surprised when Tessa had told her story. It was obvious that he was definitely hiding something.

Robbie's dreams that night were full of the drowning girl's cries for help, but when he tried to save her he couldn't see her, but the cries went on.

*

The next day all the boys met in the park. Tessa had been kept in bed, as the doctor had given her something to help her sleep. She had been traumatised, and Tommy's mother had called the doctor out very late the night before.

"She was screaming the house down," said Tommy, giving the others the details. "She definitely thinks that the other girl drowned yesterday. None of us got any sleep last night." Tommy was indeed looking very tired.

"Maybe she did," said Robbie. "Tessa seemed awfully sure that there was someone there." Robbie had a feeling that Tessa was telling the truth and that it was Frankenstein who wasn't.

"Nah," replied Tommy. "The doctor thinks that she is feeling lonely and rejected because her parents have sent her here while they wait for the new baby, and that she has invented a friend in her mind so that she has someone to talk to about things or something like that. She might just be a loony." Tommy ended on a light note. He didn't understand girls at all.

Stephen joined in at that point. "But why would she be reaching into the water if there was no one there," he said. "Why would she go into the woods in the first place? If you ask me, this imaginary friend stuff is something the doctor has made up, 'cause they can't think of anything else."

Jamie and Peter remained silent. They had missed most of the exciting bit of the adventure so they had no opinion.

"I want to go back," said Robbie, looking at the others' faces to see what kind of reaction he would get.

"To Maggie's stream! Why?" asked Tommy. He didn't want to go back there. Yesterday had been the worst day of his life.

"Because someone is lying," said Robbie, "and I can't relax until I know that a girl didn't drown. But there's more to it than that. It's the graveyard and the wood – something isn't right, and I think Frankenstein knows something. I just have a feeling. So! Who's going to come with me?"

"But we're all banned from going there," said Stephen. "How will we get past the gatehouse without Frankenstein catching us? And even if we do, there's a chance that he'll find us at the graveyard. He walks around the grounds all the time." Stephen would not admit to being just too scared to go.

"That's why I'm going to sneak down at night." Robbie was just as afraid as the rest of them, but he had to know what was going on.

"Are you nuts?" exclaimed Tommy. "After everything that happened there yesterday, you want to go back! What about the thing in the woods? Something was there, Robbie. I could feel it, the same as you felt it the night before at the graves, and you want to go there at night!" Tommy shuddered at the very thought.

"I have a plan," said Robbie. "Peter and Jamie will stay at the road before the driveway. We will give ourselves a time to be back by, and if we're not back, then they can go for help."

"Yes," said Stephen, "and how are we going to explain that to our parents? If they find out I don't think I'll ever be allowed out again!" Stephen grimaced at the thought of the lecture he had already been given by both his mother and his father, and he knew that he would be in big trouble if he disobeyed them.

"Look, all we're going to do is have a little look," said Robbie. "We won't stay for long, and if there's no sign of anything strange, then we won't ever go back, okay! So, who's coming or are you all too chicken?"

"Robbie, I must be mad, but I'm in," Tommy grinned at his friend.

"What about you, Stephen?"

"I don't know, Rob. I'll have to see if I can get out of the house. I'll try."

"Are you two okay for being lookouts then." Robbie waited for Peter and Jamie to answer.

"Well," said Jamie, "you could say you're

staying at mine, and I could say I'm staying at yours. My curfew is ten during the holidays, but that's only if I'm in the park, so we could stay here till then and leave straight from here."

"That might work, if our parents don't talk before then," replied Peter.

"We might just have to risk it, but if Peter's up for it, then so am I," said Jamie.

Robbie turned to Peter. "Well, Peter, it's up to you."

"I'm in," said Peter reluctantly. He wasn't keen, but it looked as if everyone else was going, and he and Jamie would only be keeping lookout, so it wasn't as if he had to go near the wood or the graves.

"Right, well, let's go home for lunch," said Robbie, "and we'll meet here at three to make plans."

And with that they all parted company and went back to their respective homes.

*

On returning home, Tommy went upstairs to see Tessa.

She was sitting up in bed, still looking quite

dazed from the medicine the doctor had given her, but his father had put a television in her room and she was watching cartoons.

Since her accident Tommy had softened his attitude towards his little cousin. He really thought he had lost her, and it was his concern for her that had made him go into the wood. His relief to find that she was not hurt had brought tears to his eyes.

"Hi, Tess! What are you up to?" he said softly now. Her face was still puffy from all the crying she had done, and he didn't want to set her off again.

"Just watching Tom and Jerry," said Tessa. "Did you hear anything in the village? Did anybody come looking for a little girl?"

"No, Tess," Tommy replied. "No one knows who she could be. Why don't you tell me more about her, and I'll ask some of the other kids."

"She was dressed weirdly, as if she was wearing a party dress," said Tessa, casting her mind back to the day before, "and her hair had ringlets. She had brown hair, but she didn't tell me her name. I remember, because I told her mine and I was waiting for her to tell me hers but she didn't, and I never asked. I thought maybe she didn't want to tell me."

"Why did you go off with her without telling us?"

"You were all arguing, and she just appeared, but she put a finger to her lips to tell me not to say anything. But when we got outside the graveyard she told me we would play a game of hide and seek. We would hide, and you would try to find us, and I told her you would be mad at me, but she said we would leave clues, and she put my hair-band on a branch. I didn't think she would take me so far away."

Tommy listened thoughtfully to Tessa as she finished the story of how she had ended up at the stream, trying to reach out for the other girl as she was dragged under the water. It didn't sound as if she was making it up or imagining things. She was too sure of everything, and her story had never changed. He began to think that Robbie was right. There was something going on, and if someone was telling lies, he was sure it wasn't his cousin.

"Can you remember anything else? Were you scared in the woods?" Tommy asked at last.

"I was a little, but she knew which way to go, and it didn't take long to get through the wood. I was very cold, I remember. I couldn't wait to be out in the sunshine again, but so was she, because she took my hand and her hand was really cold. I felt sorry for her. She just wanted someone to play with, and I couldn't say no."

"It's strange she didn't tell you her name," wondered Tommy.

"You don't believe me, do you!" Tessa was beginning to get upset.

"I do believe you, Tessa," replied Tommy. "Don't worry, we'll find out who she is."

Tessa was beginning to feel really sleepy but was trying so hard to stay awake because every time she closed her eyes she found herself back in the woods . . .

\*

The sun shone down on Tessa as she skipped along the path with her new friend. She didn't need those stupid boys. She would show them.

"Let's go and hide in the woods," the other

girl said, taking her by the hand and pulling her towards the trees.

Tessa felt a little frightened at the thought of going into the dark wood, but the girl beside her was so full of excitement about the game that they were going to play and totally unconcerned about going into the trees that she began to feel a bit silly over her fears, so she went along with the game.

She regretted it as soon as they entered the wood, and as they moved farther into it, the light was so poor that she began to imagine different shapes and shadows moving around her. She couldn't make out what these apparitions were. She began to panic, thinking that they were ghosts. Any moment they could get her. She gripped on to her new friend's hand, only to feel an icy coldness. She turned to look at her face, which was no longer the innocent face of a little girl but that of a wrinkled old witch, with yellow eyes and sharp teeth, blackened and rotten. Tessa let out a scream, and the creature began to laugh, a high-pitched cackle . . .

\*

"Tess, Tess, it's all right. You're safe. It was just a bad dream, darling. It's okay." Her aunt was holding her in her arms and rocking her back and forth, but Tessa couldn't speak, the dream had been too real – she couldn't get the pictures out of her head.

# Chapter 7

# *The Search Begins*

In the park later that day the boys made all their plans. Each of them was to find a way to get out of his house without arousing any suspicions, Peter and Tommy by saying they were staying at each other's, Tommy by saying that he was going to stay at Robbie's because it was easier to sneak out of Robbie's house as his parents went to bed early, and Stephen was also going to sneak out. They would meet in the park after dinner and make a plan of action.

As his mother was preparing dinner that evening Peter approached her. "Mum . . . ?" he said persuasively.

"Yes, Peter," replied Mrs Collins. "I can tell by the tone of your voice that you're after something, so out with it."

"I was just going to ask if I could stay at

Jamie's tonight. He's got a video to watch, and it's a film I haven't seen yet."

"Has he asked his mother?"

"Yes, and she said if it's okay with you then it's okay with her."

"I don't know, Peter," said his mother. "It's only the start of your holidays and already you boys have been up to all sorts of mischief. What with that little girl nearly drowning, I think I ought to be keeping a closer eye on you."

"But, Mum! exclaimed Peter. "That wasn't my fault! We never wanted a girl hanging around with us in the first place. Tommy's mother made us take her, and she just wandered off. Please, Mum, it's not like we really did anything wrong, and Jamie's mother said it's okay. I won't be any trouble, I promise. Please, please, please." He pleaded until his mother at last gave in.

"Well, Peter, I want you home first thing in the morning. It's Saturday, and your dad and I are taking you to visit your granny, okay?"

"But, Mum, there's a game of football in the park tomorrow." Peter hated visiting his granny. She always made him kiss her and treated him like a baby.

"Well, that's the deal, Peter. You can either stay here tonight and you can help your dad in the garden tomorrow, or you can go to Jamie's tonight and visit your granny tomorrow. What's it to be?"

Why couldn't he just stay at Jamie's and go to football tomorrow? But Peter knew his mother, so he agreed to come home in the morning. As soon as he had finished eating, he grabbed his PJs, towel and toothbrush, shouted goodbye to his parents and headed for the park to meet the others.

Tommy, Robbie and Jamie had already met there.

"So, what did your mum say?" Jamie asked Peter straightaway.

"Yes, she's going to let me stay, but it wasn't easy. What about you?"

"Yep! No problem."

Tommy had also had the okay to stay with Robbie. In fact, his parents thought it was a good idea. What with Tessa so upset and everything, it might do him good to get out of the house for the night.

Stephen was going to try to sneak out. "If I'm not here by eleven then you'll have to go without me," he said.

"Well, do your best, Stephen," said Robbie. "The more of us there are, the less dangerous it will be. Right! Let's make a plan."

Robbie had a pad of paper on which he had drawn a rough map of the drive and the woods, with the graveyard in between and the stream beyond the second wood.

The boys sat in the park for a while discussing the plan, and before they knew it, it was curfew and the sky was beginning to dull. It would soon be dark.

"You two should keep out of sight," said Robbie to Peter and Jamie. "Why don't you hide in the den, and we'll all meet there as close to eleven as we can."

The den was an old stable in a field next to the park, where the boys often had gang meetings. They kept sweets hidden there, and torches and other things that might come in useful on their missions, like rope and matches to light a camp-fire.

As Peter and Jamie awaited the return of the others, they talked about what lay ahead.

"Jamie, do you think those woods are really haunted?" said Peter.

"Did you see Tommy's face when we found him?" asked Jamie in reply. "Something or someone had given him a real fright, and it couldn't have been Frankenstein. He was with Robbie, so unless someone is playing a joke on us, then there's something in those trees. It might even be a tramp trying to scare us away, but he was definitely sure someone was chasing him."

"Maybe it's Robbie and Tommy playing a joke on us," said Peter.

"Maybe, but if they are then they are very good actors," replied Jamie, "and it still doesn't explain how Tessa came to be in the woods by herself, or how she fell in the water, or the fact that she swore there was another little girl when no one else saw her. No, Robbie and Tommy wouldn't have kept joking after Tessa nearly drowned."

They fell silent, each of them lost in his own thoughts.

"Jamie?" whispered Peter at last.

"Yeah?" replied Jamie.

"I'm scared," confessed Peter.

"So am I," agreed Jamie.

Once again they were silent. They had sat in silence for about ten minutes when the door burst open and Stephen entered.

"God, Stephen! You frightened the life out of me," accused Jamie.

"Sorry," said Stephen. "There were some people walking their dog in the park, and I didn't want them to see me."

"How did you manage to get out?" Peter asked.

Stephen grinned. "I made a dummy in my bed with cushions and sneaked out the back door. I'm just hoping my mother doesn't pull back the covers, because if she finds out about this, she'll kill me."

"You're mad. There's no way my mum would fall for that," Jamie said, shaking his head at Stephen.

Just then Robbie and Tommy came through the door.

"Brilliant, Stephen, you made it!" Robbie came forward and smacked Stephen on the back. "How is everyone feeling?"

"I have to tell you, I'm pretty scared," said Jamie, who didn't see the point in lying.

"Well, so am I," returned Robbie, "but you and Peter won't even have to pass the gate-house, so don't worry. You'll be okay."

"What about us, Robbie?" asked Stephen. "None of us has any idea what's out there. What if we find something, what will we do?"

"We're just going to have to see what happens," replied Robbie. "There might not be anything there. It might have been animals or an overactive imagination that has made us think there is something in the woods. I mean, none of us has even seen anything."

"But what if there is something?" asked Stephen. What if we get caught? What if someone gets hurt? This is serious – we have to have a plan."

"That's why we have to put a time limit on

the time we spend there," said Robbie. "If we're not back in one and a half hours then Jamie and Peter go for help. I mean it, guys. Don't hesitate – just run and get someone as fast as you can, but not Mr Bowman. Don't forget, he could be in on this."

"Okay," said Peter, "but what if you're not in trouble and we go and get help and then we all get into trouble?" Peter was thinking about the punishment his parents would inflict on him if he were caught, and it wasn't a pleasant thought.

"That's a chance we're going to have to take," said Robbie, taking a deep breath. "Is everyone ready?"

They all nodded, although none of them felt ready to do what he was about to do.

The walk through the fields was difficult in the dark. The ground was bumpy, and each of them tripped a few times, but it was the quickest route, and there was no traffic, so no one would see them if they happened to drive by. Once they were on the road, however, they would have to crouch in the trees at the side. If any cars went by, they couldn't risk anyone seeing them.

They were lucky. The road was very quiet, and once they were a few feet from the Priory driveway and could see the lights from the gatehouse they stopped.

"Okay, Jamie, Peter," whispered Robbie. "Hide in the long grass here, and don't make too much noise, and, of course, don't let anyone in passing cars see you." Robbie was talking as quietly as he could. "It's half-past eleven. If we're not back here by one o'clock, get help. Tell them we're in the woods at the other side of the graveyard. Tommy, have you got the string?"

Tommy produced a large ball of string from his rucksack and handed it to Robbie.

"When we get to the far side of the graveyard," continued Robbie, "we're going to tie this string to the first tree, and then every few trees after that, so that we won't get lost, and if we need help you'll be able to find us easily, okay?"

He looked at the frightened faces of his friends. "Let's go!" he said. "Remember, one o'clock!" Then he, Tommy and Stephen crept away into the night.

They crept silently forward, ducking into the thick bushes at the side of the road. There were lights on in the gatehouse, but they felt confident that Frankenstein had not seen them.

Once they felt they had reached a safe distance from the gatehouse they moved into the road and continued on until they came to the little wooden gate. There they stopped outside, each of them wanting to delay going any farther. The night was so quiet and still that all they could hear was the occasional hoot of an owl and their own hearts hammering in their chests. Had they made a mistake? Would they have the courage to enter the woods and the graveyard beyond?

No one spoke. They just stood quietly contemplating the journey before them, afraid of what they might find in this dark mysterious place, a place of secrets, secrets that perhaps they did not want to know.

"It seems pretty quiet in there," said Stephen. "Maybe we should just go home."

Stephen had been the most reluctant from the start but did not want to be the only one to be thought of as a coward.

"We've come this far. We may as well find out if there's anything in there." Robbie sounded as if he had no fear of the woods, but inside he half hoped that the others would persuade him to go no farther.

Tommy thought of his little cousin. She would never be able to forget the little girl who, she was sure, had been drowned. Her life would be ruined by the guilt she felt that she had not been able to save her. If he could find out what really had happened that day then he had to do it, for her sake. He reached forward and pushed open the gate, and, with just a little hesitation, stepped through and into the trees. Then he turned to his friends. "Let's get this over with."

Tommy's new-found bravery was all the encouragement that the other boys needed, so with a shrug they followed him into the woods. None of them spoke or made any other sound for fear that he would alert the inhabitants of the wood to his presence.

The walk through the first wood of trees was uneventful. Apart from the occasional hoot of an owl, they saw or heard nothing, and by the time they got to the iron gate of the graveyard they were feeling a lot more confident. Although none of them was in a great hurry to open the gate, this time Robbie took the lead, and the gate creaked slowly open.

"Look! Over there! What's that?" Stephen was pointing at a dark shape slouched across a grave. It was Margaret Grainger's grave.

"It looks like a body," said Robbie. "Have you got a torch, Tommy?"

Robbie took the torch from the other boy and slowly made his way across the graveyard, cautiously afraid of what he might find, edging forward until he was standing next to the grave. He shone the light on the dark object. "It's Frankenstein!" he exclaimed.

"Is he dead?" Tommy asked, his voice shaking.

"I don't know." Robbie replied, leaning forward and peering at the old man's face. Then Mr Bowman's eyes opened suddenly, giving the boy a fright, and he jumped back.

"Get away, boy, while you can," the old man urged in barely a whisper.

"Are you okay, Mr Bowman? What happened?" asked Robbie anxiously.

Robbie saw that there was blood coming from a cut on the old man's head.

"Never mind me," replied the gatekeeper. "You have to get out of here, before *she* comes. Quickly! It's not safe."

Mr Bowman seemed to have recovered a little of his strength and was pushing Robbie away.

"Who's coming?" asked Robbie. "We can't just leave you here like this. You're hurt."

Once more Robbie moved forward and tried to help the gatekeeper to his feet, but the old man looked past Robbie and his eyes widened with fear.

Behind him, Robbie could hear a strange hissing noise. Turning to look, he encountered a strange mist seeping through the gate, slowly coming towards them.

Tommy and Stephen followed the direction of his eyes and jumped towards Robbie, the three of them close together as the mist advanced on them. The whole graveyard filled with cold air, and as the seconds passed the boys froze in fear, not knowing where the mist had come from, only that it was bad, judging by Mr Bowman's reaction to it.

"What is it?" asked Stephen.

"Its her! She's come for me. You'll have to go out through the other gate. Go now," Mr Bowman ordered, but the boys could not move, as that same childish laughter that they had heard in the graveyard filled the enclosure, and a little girl appeared from the mist . . .

# Chapter 8

# *Meeting Maggie*

The little girl walked slowly towards them, and although she looked like any little girl from a distance, as she came closer to them, Robbie could see that there was no life in her face, just a blank expression.

The old gatekeeper was the first to speak: "Maggie, leave them alone. You have enough friends, you don't need them."

But still she came forward, her dead eyes staring at the man on the ground. She spoke: "I will have any friends I like, old man, and you will no longer try to stop me." She laughed softly, and the mist came forward again.

The three boys backed away as it covered Mr Bowman's legs, but the old man began to dig at the grave with his hands. Frantically searching for something, he ploughed at the earth, but the mist was almost covering him, depleting his strength. As it reached his neck, he found what he was looking for and held the object towards Robbie, who quickly grabbed it from his out-stretched hand. Robbie wiped the dirt off it and saw that it was a statue of an angel. It looked as if it was made of tarnished silver, but what did it mean?

The mist was moving over Robbie's head, and he started to choke, but Mr Bowman croaked out instructions to him: "Take it to the stream. Run as fast as you can. Don't stop. You have to throw it in the water. Go! Go!" He was coughing and gasping for air as if he was suffo-cating.

Robbie gave him one last look, turned and ran out of the back entrance of the graveyard. He thought about the string that Tommy had, but there was no time. He just ran straight into the wood, which would take him to Maggie's stream. On and on he ran, hoping against hope that he was going in the right direction. His face was stinging as he pushed his way through the branches. It was as if the trees were attacking him, but somehow he gathered the strength not to stop. Even when he thought he could run no more, he managed to carry on. He was running for his life.

At last Robbie heard the sound of running water, but at the same time he also heard the distinct hissing sound of the mist and the accompanying laughter of the ghost of Maggie Grainger. He didn't dare look behind him. He just knew these strange manifestations were gaining on him.

He could see just a little trickle of moonlight and knew he was almost at the other side of the wood, so he pushed himself that little bit harder. Only when he was about to leave the wood did he dare to look behind him and was shocked to see that the mist was almost on top of him. He looked ahead again, but not in time to save himself from tripping over a fallen branch. He landed on his face, and felt the icy finger of the mist closing round his ankle.

As he tried to drag himself to his feet, still clutching the little silver angel, he clawed at the ground with his other hand, using his fingers as an anchor to stop the mist from pulling him in.

Somehow Robbie found the strength to shake off the grip of the mist. He scrambled to his feet and turned to run towards the stream. He was almost there when he heard the sound of laughter and turned to see the child ghost emerging from the mist.

"Would you like to play a game?" It was not the voice of a little girl but that of a witch, and when he looked at her face he could see that she now looked like an old crow. Her voice rose to a cackle as she screamed and laughed.

Robbie couldn't move. He was rooted to the spot as the creature came towards him, with the menacing mist at her feet as if it was her pet. She was almost upon him when he came to his senses. Without hesitation, he made one last run for the stream, and without stopping to think he threw the angel as far as he could out into the water. As soon as it hit its target, he was surrounded by a horrible agonised scream as the water rose and the screaming ghost was pulled and sucked deep into the stream. The ground shook, the water frothed and bubbled, and then, suddenly, there was silence, and the water was still.

Robbie lost consciousness and fell to the ground.

# Chapter 9

# *All is Explained*

Robbie came round to find his father and some of the other village people, as well as the local police, around him. It seemed that Jamie and Peter had gone for help when the other three had not returned. Stephen and Tommy had been found with Mr Bowman shortly after Robbie had run off with the angel, so what seemed like a lifetime had only been about ten minutes. The others must have already told most of the story to the grown-ups, because his father just wrapped Robbie in a blanket and led him through the wood, past the graveyard, back to the road to a waiting car, where the local doctor was waiting to check him over.

"He's in shock, but apart from a few scrapes and bruises there don't seem to be any other in-juries," said the doctor. "The best thing we can do is get him home to bed and keep him warm. I'll give him something to help him sleep."

All the grown-ups were whispering to each other, all wondering what on earth had happened. The story they had heard so far seemed a bit hard to believe, but something had happened to frighten the boys, and old Mr Bowman had been unconscious and driven straight to hospital in a nearby town.

Robbie's dad assured them that he would question his son the next day and would be sure to fill them in with every detail, but right now he had to get him home.

It took the village a few days to settle down after the news of the boys' adventure had spread. Everyone was talking, and there were a few different versions of the story. Some people believed the stories, and others laughed it off as young boys with overactive imaginations.

Mr Bowman was recovering in hospital but had asked too see Robbie and Tommy, so Robbie's father drove them into town and left them with the old man, who looked so fragile, lying in the hospital bed. His face was bruised and weary, but he looked pleased to see the two boys and ushered them to sit beside his bed.

Robbie produced some biscuits that his mother had made and handed them to the old man, who whispered his thanks, and, clearing his throat, began to speak. "I'm glad you came. I have wanted to both apologise and to thank you for what you did that night."

"It's okay, Mr Bowman. You have nothing to apologise for. We shouldn't have been there in the first place. Our parents are still a bit sore at us for disobeying them." Robbie hurried to assure the gatekeeper that he was not to blame for what had happened that night. He felt sorry for him. He looked so old and tired, not the same man they had all been so afraid of.

"Yes I do" replied the old man, "which is why I'm going to tell you the whole truth. I'm going to tell you the story of Maggie Grainger, then you might understand better."

The boys said nothing. They very much wanted to know about Maggie. There were so many questions still unanswered.

"I began working at the Priory when I was

just a young man of twenty," Mr Bowman began. "My first position was as a junior gardener. At that time there was a huge staff. In those days we didn't have all the machinery they have now. Everything was done by hand, so there were five or six gardeners then, and I very quickly became aware of the stories that the staff used to tell to each other about ghosts. It seemed that just about everyone who worked or lived in the place had at one time or another seen a ghost, but I didn't really take the tales too seriously at first. Most of them were in the house anyway, but the gardeners had their own ghost, and all of them swore that they had seen her – a little girl.

"There were many different tales. Some had just glimpsed her hiding behind trees, some had seen her walking through the gate at the old graveyard. Some had heard laughter, but there wasn't one of the gardeners who didn't believe in her."

He paused, and gave a meaningful look at the boys. "I didn't know whether I believed the stories or not," he continued, "until I met her for the first time. I thought she was a relative of the big house. She was skipping along one of the paths one day, laughing and singing. I never thought anything of it until I mentioned it to one of the other gardeners, who told me that it couldn't be anyone from the house as all the family had gone to visit relatives in England for a holiday. He asked me to describe the child, which I did, and he told me that it was her, the ghost. I was amazed, but somehow I knew he was right, and that was the first of many times that I saw her."

Mr Bowman leaned over and took a drink from the water glass at the side of his bed while Tommy and Robbie eagerly waited for him to continue his story.

"I just carried on as normal," he went on, leaning back against his pillows. "She never did any harm, so the gardeners just accepted her. No one was really afraid of her. Then the body of a child was found in Maggie's stream, and I got to hear even more stories from the past. This wasn't the first time that children had drowned in the stream, and people had become superstitious about it. There were no fish in it, ever, and it was not a place children would want to swim, so what drew them to the stream nobody knew, so I asked a few questions.

"The stream was named after a little girl who had drowned there in the 1800s. She had been an only child, and a very lonely one. Her parents didn't approve of their daughter mixing with the village children. In their eyes the local children weren't good enough for Margaret, so she was banned from playing with them. No matter how much she begged her parents to let her make friends, they were not welcomed at the Priory, so young Maggie spent her days trying to amuse herself, inventing games and trying her best to make the most of her own company. It was while she was on her own one day that she fell into the water and drowned."

Robbie and Tommy felt sorry for the lonely little girl, who had died so unhappily.

"Her parents must have blamed themselves," said Robbie, thoughtfully. "If they had only allowed Maggie to make friends with the village children, then maybe she would never have been playing alone next to the water, and they would not have lost their only child. So that is what the poem on her gravestone means?"

Mr Bowman nodded. "Yes, I'm sure that's what it means, but I still couldn't work out why so many children were drowning in that stream. Over the years parents had begun to forbid their children to go near the stream, but still something seemed to attract them to it, and still there were accidents. I stumbled on the reason quite accidentally."

Mr Bowman stopped to take another drink of water before continuing: "I was keeping an eye on some local children who were exploring the grounds. We had been having trouble with vandalism, so I followed them to make sure that they were not the culprits, and when they went into the graveyard I hid and watched. One young boy wandered outside the wall, near to where I was hiding, when Maggie appeared. She lured him into the woods, telling him they would play hide and seek, and he went with her into the woods. He never came back. His body was found later on that day, by me, and that was when I realised what she was doing. She was making the friends she had never had a chance to make before, but to keep them she was somehow making them fall into the stream, then they would be her friends for eternity.

"It was hard to believe, but after that I kept a close watch on the stream, and managed to stop most children from going there, but the more I tried to save them, the more she seemed to make the whole thing into a game. I'm almost seventy-six years old. I have spent fifty-six years of my life trying to protect children from the ghost of Margaret Grainger, with no idea how long I could keep going, or if she would ever stop."

It was an amazing story, but after the boys thought it through it all began to make sense.

Maggie must have been trying to drown Tessa. Mr Bowman was not there by coincidence. He knew what was going to happen. That was also why they had always felt that he was watching them, but he was trying to keep them safe, not to scare them. Everything was beginning to fall into place, apart from . . .

"But how did you know about the angel," asked Robbie. "How could you know that it would stop her?"

"I didn't, not really. It was just a lucky guess," replied Mr Bowman. "The Priory has records of every birth and death, and a history of the family and all who are buried in that graveyard. It also mentions some of the old traditions, one of which is the burying of statues with their loved ones. The Graingers believed that a silver statue of an angel would guard the soul, so I checked the grave of Maggie, and there it was, but I put it back. It didn't feel right, removing it from the grave, and I didn't know how significant it was at the time. It was only when I thought that she was going to kill us all that I thought that if the family were right and these angels held the souls of the dead then, perhaps, to remove the angel might destroy her. I just guessed that throwing it into the water she drowned in might be the ideal place for it. I wasn't sure it would work. I was desperate, but once you had taken the angel I knew she was afraid, and I prayed harder than I have ever done in my life that you would make it to that stream. So thank you, son. If you hadn't been so fast and brave I dread to think what could have happened, but I still have to apologise to you and your friends. If I hadn't kept her secrets to myself for so long, I could maybe have found a way to stop her sooner. I was a silly old man."

There were tears in the old man's eyes and he looked so defeated that Robbie and Tommy felt really sorry for him. They tried their best to re-assure him that they didn't blame him. After all, no one had been hurt apart from Mr Bowman, and, in fact, they had had a great adventure, not one they wanted to repeat, but, all the same, now that they knew the full story, it was a tale they could tell for years to come.

Robbie's father arrived to take the boys home, so they said goodbye to Mr Bowman and asked if they could visit him again, which seemed to please the old man.

On the way home they told Mr Brown the whole tale, and he agreed that it was an amaz-ing ghost story, but added that he hoped that they had had enough adventure for one summer holiday, to which they returned that they had had enough adventure for a lifetime.

The boys all met in the park that evening, where Tommy and Robbie once more repeated the story that Mr Bowman had told them.

"It's hard to believe, even though I was there. It's like I dreamed it. Who would have thought that we would go on a ghost hunt and actually find a real ghost," grinned Stephen, and they all burst out laughing.

"I know what you mean, " said Robbie. "It was the last thing I expected. How's Tessa?" He turned to Tommy, changing the subject.

"She's much better, thanks," Tommy replied. "Mum told her a little, just enough to reassure her but not enough to frighten her, so the nightmares have almost stopped completely."

Tommy had spent a lot of time with his young cousin, watching films and playing games, to take her mind of things. And soon she would be going home, as Tessa's mother would be having the new baby any day now, and with a new brother or sister to fuss after, she was bound to forget all about her awful experience.

The boys talked for a little while longer. Robbie began to tell them what had happened after he had run into the woods, and the others all sat in awe, impressed at how brave he had been, but he shrugged it all off. He had not felt brave. He had been scared out of his wits, but it was all over now, and when they started to make arrangements to meet the next day they were all in agreement on what they wanted to do.

"Football!" they shouted in unison.

A nice quiet game of football – no graves, no woods, no stream and, most of all, no spooks.

*

A new story came about after word of the children's adventure spread around the village. Now, in the summertime, it is said that if you stare into the stream in the moonlight it is not your own reflection you will see, but that of the little girl they used to call Maggie.

THE END

# Other titles in this series:

## *Captured in the Castle*
**Felix Bogarte**

Ever wanted to know what it's like to be a ghost? Well, this is the story of David and Simon, two lads who became ghosts – and then wished they hadn't! On a school trip to Linchester Castle, our heroes agree to lend their bodies to two ghosts trapped there. The ghosts promise to swap back before the class leaves the castle. Would you fall for that one? Read this spooky tale and discover what happens when you make deals with ghosts.

## *River of Blood*
**Felix Bogarte**

Ever wondered where the expression "Kilroy was here" came from? If you believe this ghost story, you'll discover the answer lies in the bizarre past of an old ship. Paul and Tommy befriend a quirky American tourist who claims to be a psychic detective exploring a ghostly legend. The boys wonder at how much he knows about ghosts and how he explains the mysterious goings on that have baffled the city of Linchester over the past weeks.

## *Treasure Hunt*

### Rachel Morrison

Robbie is a normal boy leading a normal life – but all that is about to change! He receives a strange parcel on his twelfth birthday, and suddenly he and his friend are transported to a strange tropical island that is not on any map and is inhabited by weird creatures, scary pirates and glorious mermaids. Robbie and his friend discover that there is treasure on the island and are determined not to leave without it, no matter how scared they get!